It's a Mummy!

The Hounds tiptoed into the room.

"This place is like a scene from the movie *The Mummy's Curse*." Stanley shuddered.

Against one wall was a giant throne and a painting of a pyramid. Nearby was a pair of mummies, their bandages frayed and yellowed. Next to a cluttered old desk were piles of clean, white bandages.

Stanley sat down on the pile while Alkali and Rose searched the room.

Suddenly Stanley felt a kick. His eyes got round as saucers, and he shot to his feet.

"The bandages!" yelled Rose. "They're moving!"

"I've got news for you," said Alkali. "That's not just a pile of bandages."

They watched in horror as the pile of rags began rolling their way.

"Oh, no!" screamed Stanley. "Run for your lives. It's a mummy!"

THE MUMMY'S SECRET

by Stephen Mooser

Illustrated by Leslie Morrill

Troll Associates

This book is for
Sue Alexander.

Library of Congress Cataloging in Publication Data

Mooser, Stephen.
   The mummy's secret.

   (Treasure hounds)
   Summary: When they discover mysterious hieroglyphics
on the back of a photograph encased in an old locket,
the three Shadow Beach Treasure Hounds determine to
find out what they mean.
   [1. Mystery and detective stories. 2. Buried
treasure—Fiction] I. Morrill, Leslie H., ill.
II. Title. III. Series: Mooser, Stephen. Treasure
hounds.
PZ7.M78817Mu   1988   [Fic]   87-16152
ISBN 0-8167-1181-X (lib. bdg.)
ISBN 0-8167-1182-8 (pbk.)

A TROLL BOOK, published by Troll Associates,
Mahwah, NJ 07430

Contents

The Locket

THE SHADOW BEACH JUNIOR HIGH SCHOOL cafeteria was one of the noisiest spots in the world, especially at lunch time. Carrying on a conversation amid the banging trays, booming loudspeaker announcements, and shouts of students, cooks, and teachers was never easy. Still, the Shadow Beach Treasure Hounds—namely, Rose Flint, Stanley Duggins, and Alkali Jones—almost daily held a meeting in the center of the room while eating lunch.

The cafeteria was one of the few places where they could talk about their treasure-hunting business. For more than a year, the three of them had been helping people find their lost valuables. Already they'd located a missing safe, an old mine, and once, even a cave full of stolen goods.

On that day, Alkali Jones was telling Rose and Stanley about the Dutch Oven Gold, missing riches he'd just read about in his favorite magazine, *True Treasure*. Suddenly, they were interrupted by one of their classmates, Bunny Ferguson, a wild-eyed girl with bright red lips and frizzy hair.

"Pssst!" she said, leaning over Alkali's shoulder. "Wanna buy a giant diamond?"

Alkali turned around and tipped back his cowboy hat with a solitary finger.

"Huh?" he shouted over the clatter in the room. "What did you say?"

Bunny looked about the room as if someone might be spying on her. "Wanna buy a diamond?" she asked louder.

Stanley Duggins, his long, freckled face buried in a hamburger dripping with ketchup, was so busy eating he hadn't even noticed Bunny. But Rose had. "What?" she said, leaning across the table and narrowing her bright green eyes.

Bunny looked around again and said louder still "A diamond. I'm selling a one-pound diamond at my yard sale after school today."

"A one-pound diamond?" Alkali said skeptically.

"Since you guys are always after treasure, I thought you might be interested. My mother just finished her spring cleaning, and everything she doesn't want she said I could sell."

"How much are you selling the diamond for?" asked Rose.

"Five bucks," said Bunny. "It's a real bargain."

"It sounds like it," said Rose. "Bunny, a diamond that size would be worth a million dollars, at least."

"A million dollars?" said Stanley, looking up from his sandwich, a streak of ketchup on his cheek. "Where?"

Rose pointed at Bunny. "Our friend here is selling a million-dollar diamond for five bucks," she said.

"Wow," said Stanley, "that sounds like a great deal!"

Rose rolled her eyes. "Stanley, I swear, you are so gullible. Do you really think Bunny has a one-pound diamond for sale? Diamonds that size are all in museums, under twenty-four-hour guard."

Bunny put her hands on her hips and glared across the table. An announcement about an afternoon assembly was coming over the loudspeaker, so Bunny had to shout to be heard. "Are you coming or not?"

Rose didn't believe for a second that Bunny's diamond was real, but she was curious about what else the girl might be selling. Rose believed that treasure, like beauty, was often in the eye of the beholder. And she just might find something of a treasure in Bunny Ferguson's front yard.

"We'll be there after school!" she shouted.

By the time the Hounds got to the sale that afternoon, Bunny had already laid everything out on a blanket in the middle of her front yard. Most of the stuff looked like junk, but Bunny presented each item as if it were a valuable antique.

"Only ten cents for this rare brush," she said, displaying a worn, plastic hairbrush. "I happen to know that this was once owned by Abraham Lincoln."

"Bunny, really," said Rose, "it's a scientific fact that plastic wasn't invented when Lincoln was alive."

Bunny shrugged her shoulders. "If you don't want it, just say so," she said. "But, please, don't put down my fine merchandise in front of the other customers."

"What about that diamond?" asked Stanley.

"Right here," said Bunny, picking up a big piece of quartz. "A genuine diamond. Only five bucks, and it's yours."

"That's just a rock," said Stanley. "Even I can see that."

"I believe a jeweler would say otherwise," said Bunny. She set down the sparkling rock and picked up a large copper locket in the shape of a beetle. "How about this, then?"

Stanley looked over her shoulder as Bunny snapped open the locket. Inside was a very old picture of a young woman in a wide bonnet.

"My mother bought this years ago at a junk store," she said. "I don't have the slightest idea whose picture is in it, but I'm sure she was somebody famous. Otherwise she couldn't have afforded such a valuable piece of jewelry. This metal, of course, is worth a small fortune."

Stanley tilted his head. "A *small* fortune is right! Since when was copper so valuable?"

Bunny looked about, then lowered her voice. "Only looks like copper. I happen to know that this locket is made out of pure callium."

"Callium? Never heard of it," said Stanley.

"Few people have," said Bunny. "They haven't made it in fifty years. That's why it's so rare." She winked. "What do you say, Stanley? Will you give me fifty cents for it?"

"Nice try," said Stanley, "but I don't think so."

"But I will," said Rose, reaching over Bunny's shoulder and grabbing the locket. "I've been looking for something like this for a long time."

"It's fifty cents," said Bunny. "According to my mother, it's made out of pure septium, the most valuable metal in the world."

"I thought you just said it was made out of something called callium?" said Stanley.

Bunny dismissed Stanley with a wave of her hand, "Details, details," she said. "It's still a bargain."

"It is," said Rose, although she had no idea what an incredible bargain it would turn out to be.

2

A Mysterious Message

THE FIRST THING ROSE DID when she got home with the locket was to remove the picture of the lady in the wide bonnet.

"I'm not going to carry around a picture of a lady I've never met," she said out loud. "Instead, I'm going to put in a picture of a man I've never met: Mel Fisher, the greatest treasure hunter of the twentieth century."

The yellowed picture came out easily with the aid of a letter opener. Before tossing it into the trash, Rose glanced at the back and was surprised to see that it was covered with tiny symbols.

"It looks like Egyptian hieroglyphics," she murmured. And after a careful examination with the aid of a magnifying glass, Rose was convinced that that was exactly what they were.

The next day at school, she showed the markings to Alkali and Stanley.

"Looks like a treasure map," said Alkali immediately. His mind was on treasure nearly one hundred percent of the time. Everything he looked at had some connection with a treasure he'd either read or heard about. "Probably a guide to the secret chambers of an ancient pyramid."

Rose gave Alkali a skeptical look. "I didn't know you could read old Egyptian writing," she said.

"Merely an educated guess," said Alkali. "I mean, really, what else could it be, considering the way it was hidden?"

"I think we ought to show this to my history teacher, Mrs. Perkus," said Stanley. "She knows all about Egyptian history. Maybe she'll be able to figure out what it says."

After school, the three Hounds stopped by Mrs. Perkus's room and showed her the hieroglyphics on the back of the photo. As it turned out, Mrs. Perkus, a tall, gray-haired woman with erect posture, didn't have the foggiest notion of the meaning of the hieroglyphics. But she did know who might.

"As it happens, tomorrow night I'm attending a meeting of the Shadow Beach Order of the Sphinx, an organization devoted to the study of ancient Egypt," she said. "The main speaker, Mr. Ramses Orion, is an expert on hieroglyphics. I'm sure he'd be more than happy to translate this for you."

"Ramses Orion?" said Stanley. "Isn't he that weird guy who walks around town in those gold robes?"

Mrs. Perkus nodded. "Mr. Orion believes he is a direct descendant of King Tutankhamen," she said. "Yes, I suppose he does dress a little strangely."

"A little!" said Alkali. "Pardner, that guy is plumb loco. No way I'm handing over that map."

"Map?" said Mrs. Perkus.

Rose laughed. "Alkali's wishful thinking," she said.

Mrs. Perkus gathered up her books. "If you decide to come, the meeting will be held at Sphinx Hall at seven o'clock." She headed for the door, then paused briefly before going out. "By the way, Mr. Orion's talk tomorrow will be entitled 'How to Make a Mummy.'"

Stanley gulped and nearly dropped his own book. "Mu—mu—mu—mummy. He's going to make a real live mummy!"

Rose smiled. "Stanley, I think you've seen too many monster movies. Mummies aren't alive. They're people who have been dead for thousands of years."

"Ever see *The Mummy's Curse*?" asked Stanley. "That guy was not dead."

"It was only a movie, Stanley," said Rose. She looked at Alkali and smiled. "I think Stanley believes everything he sees on TV."

"This Orion guy is crazy," Stanley continued. "Who knows what kinds of things go on at those meetings? Forget it. I'm not going."

"Of course you're going," said Rose. "You're a Treasure Hound. We've got to stick together."

"Not this time," said Stanley. "Mummies and I definitely do not get along. No way. Not for a million dollars."

Alkali chuckled. "How about for two million, then? Or even two billion?"

"Billion?" said Stanley. "What are you talking about?"

"I'm talking about the treasure we're trying to track down," said Alkali. "Those old Egyptians buried tons of gold and jewels." He looked at Stanley and winked. "And we're hot on the trail of some of it. I can't believe you'd consider dropping out now."

Stanley rubbed his chin and thought. "Billions, you say?"

"Maybe even more," said Alkali. "This is big, Stanley. Real big."

"Well," said Stanley, "as long as you put it that way."

Rose slapped Stanley on the back. "I knew you wouldn't let us down."

"That Orion guy is creepy," said Stanley. "Billions or not, I wish we didn't have to show him the map."

"What are our choices?" said Rose. "Orion is the only person in town who can read the message on the back of the photo."

"Nevertheless, we'll have to be careful," said Alkali. "I don't like the idea of showing the whole thing to Mr. Orion either. How will we know if he gives us the right translation?"

Rose nodded. Alkali did have a point. "I'll tell you what. To be on the safe side, I'll make a copy of the message, tear it in two, and just let him see one half. We'll see what he says, then go on from there."

"I like that idea," said Alkali. "Just let him see a little bit of it till we figure out whether he's trustworthy. One thing we don't need now is trouble."

"Don't worry," said Rose. "There won't be any trouble."

But Rose couldn't have been more mistaken. For trouble was waiting, big trouble. And it would all start the following night at seven o'clock in Sphinx Hall.

17

3

The Shadow Beach Order of the Sphinx

AT SEVEN O'CLOCK THE NEXT EVENING, the Treasure Hounds met outside a white, two-story building with a pointed, gold roof, Sphinx Hall. As the Hounds watched, members of the Shadow Beach Order of the Sphinx arrived and stood on the steps leading into the building. They talked among themselves and exchanged weird handshakes, which involved the tapping together of each other's elbows.

"Must be some kind of ancient Egyptian greeting," whispered Alkali. He looked over the crowd, many of whom were dressed in golden robes plastered with purple images of pyramids, sphinxes, and floating eyes. "Looks like these people take their club seriously."

Before long a gong sounded, and the members of the Order of the Sphinx filed up the stairs and into Sphinx Hall. The three Treasure Hounds followed them and eventually found themselves seated on folding chairs inside the hall's main room. They waited nervously for the start of the evening's program.

There were about thirty other people, including Mrs. Perkus, gathered beneath the hall's high ceiling. They were talking excitedly among themselves about their mutual interest: the old kingdoms on the Nile. There was no doubt that the members of the Order of the Sphinx were great fans of ancient Egypt. Pictures of the Sphinx—a huge lionlike figure with a human face—and the pyramids decorated the walls, and the gold ceiling was covered with hieroglyphics. At the front of the large room, atop a shiny black table, were what looked like enough bandages to equip an entire hospital.

"What do you think those bandages are for?" asked Stanley suspiciously. "They look pretty awful."

"I'm sure Ramses Orion will tell us all about them," said Rose. She glanced over her shoulder. "Here he comes now."

A hush fell over the crowd as Ramses Orion, a balding man sporting a pencil-thin mustache and golden robes, strode up to the table and called the meeting to order.

"Greetings!" he said. "On behalf of the ancient kings of Egypt, I bid you welcome!"

"Greetings, Ramses!" the crowd replied.

"Are you prepared to learn the mysteries of the Sphinx?" he asked.

"Yes, teach us," they all replied.

Stanley looked around for the nearest exit. As far as he could tell, the people in the Shadow Beach Order of the Sphinx were a bunch of kooks. If things started getting crazy, he had no intention of sticking around.

Mr. Orion began the evening with a straightfor-

ward explanation of the importance the Egyptians placed on the preservation of the body after death. He said that, even to this day, people still didn't know all the secrets of mummy making.

"This isn't so scary," whispered Stanley. "It sounds just like school."

Mr. Orion raised his hands above his head, then swayed about for a while, singing in some foreign language. The lecture part of the program had clearly ended.

Suddenly, slapping his hands down on the table, he cried, "Let us begin!" Ramses Orion scanned the audience with his tiny, black eyes, finally letting them settle on Stanley. "You, there," he said, pointing, "come. I need a volunteer to help me demonstrate the ancient art of mummy making."

Stanley looked around, hoping that Mr. Orion had pointed at someone else, but when he saw everyone's eyes looking his way, he figured out the awful truth and slumped into his chair.

Orion gestured with his finger. "Come, my boy," he said, "you should feel honored. The kings of Egypt are calling you."

"With all due respect to the kings," said Stanley, "I wish you would choose someone else."

Orion narrowed his eyes. "How can you refuse such an honor?"

Rose jabbed Stanley in the ribs with her elbow. "Go on. Don't make a scene."

"I don't see you volunteering," said Stanley.

"I wasn't asked," said Rose. "Now go on. We're guests here."

"Yeah," whispered Alkali, "you're insulting these people. Go on. Get up there."

"I'm waiting," said Mr. Orion.

Stanley glared at Alkali and Rose, then slowly got to his feet.

Mr. Orion smiled. "Come," he said, gesturing toward Stanley, "I promise you this won't hurt a bit."

Stanley took his time getting to the front of the room. Every few steps, he looked back over his shoulder at Alkali and Rose, but each time his two partners just waved for him to keep going.

"Tell me," said Ramses Orion, rubbing his hands together, "what do they call you in this life?"

Stanley gulped. "This life?"

Ramses smiled. "All of us here have lived many lives—you, too, my boy."

For a moment Stanley considered bolting for the door. Orion was nuttier than a tree full of acorns.

"Your name," repeated Ramses, "please."

"Stanley Duggins," said Stanley softly. He looked at Ramses and lowered his voice still further. "This won't take long, I hope. My mother is expecting me soon."

"This will take only a few minutes," said Mr. Orion. He waved his hand over the table. "Please, Stanley, won't you lie down."

Stanley sighed, looked at Rose and Alkali again, and did as he was told.

Ramses Orion then proceeded to wave his hands over Stanley, all the while chanting some mumbo jumbo about Nefertiti, the famous Egyptian queen, and the tombs of the Pharaohs.

Then, suddenly, just as everyone had begun to

wonder what all this had to do with making mummies, Ramses seized the pile of bandages, and in a series of quick motions punctuated by shouts and cries, he wrapped up Stanley from head to toe.

"Done!" cried Ramses, raising his hands into the air like a victorious prizefighter. "And in world-record time, too."

For a few moments the room was silent save for the muffled cries of poor Stanley. Wrapped up like a caterpillar in a cocoon, he was bouncing up and down on the table. The crowd erupted into cheers and shouts, which Mr. Orion modestly acknowledged with a bow and wave of his hand.

It must have been at least five minutes more before Orion undid the bandages and freed Stanley. The second the bonds were off, Stanley leaped from the table and dashed back to his seat, without so much as a word to anyone in the room.

"That wasn't so bad, was it?" said Alkali, leaning over.

Stanley shook his head. His face was the color of chalk. "I'm never, ever listening to you guys again. That was horrible."

Rose smiled. "Really? From here it looked like fun."

Stanley glared at Rose. "I'm going to get you for this, Rose Flint. Someday."

The meeting dragged on for nearly an hour as the members of the Sphinx club discussed the merits of building a pyramid just outside of town to serve as their new headquarters. After they appointed a committee to look into the matter, the meeting was adjourned.

Making their way to the front of the room, the Treasure Hounds approached Ramses Orion as he was bent over the table, carefully folding up the bandages.

"Excuse me," said Rose, clearing her throat. "I wonder if we might have a few moments of your time."

Mr. Orion looked up and smiled. "Of course, my dear. What is it?"

Rose reached into her pocket, drew out the slip of paper that contained half the hieroglyphics, and handed it to Mr. Orion. "My friends and I were wondering if you could tell us what these symbols mean," she said. "We're dying of curiosity."

"I don't usually do this sort of thing," Orion said, examining the hieroglyphics. "However, since Stanley was such a big help to me tonight—" Suddenly he glanced up and fixed Rose with his tiny black eyes. "Where—where did you get this?"

"I, ummm, found it," said Rose.

Wrinkling his brow, he read through the note once more.

"What does it say?" asked Alkali.

"The mere scribblings of a schoolgirl," said Orion calmly. "A love note, nothing more."

"Who is it from? Whom is it for?" asked Stanley.

Orion glanced down at the paper. "I wouldn't know because it's only partly here." He looked again at Rose and narrowed his eyes. "Young lady, where's the rest of it?"

Rose shrugged her shoulders and took a step back.

Ramses pointed a long, bony finger at her. "I asked you a question. Where's the rest of this note?"

While Rose was considering her reply, Alkali said, "If it's just a love note, what does it matter? Why are you so interested in seeing more?"

Orion drew back his head and let a tiny smile form on his lips.

"It's just that I'm interested in all things Egyptian," he said as Rose took back the piece of paper. "If there is more to the note, and I assume there is, I'd like to take a peek at it."

Rose nodded. "You're right, there is more." She patted a pocket on her blouse. "But for now it's going to stay right in here. There's some more research we'd like to do first."

Orion reached out and clamped a bony hand on Rose's shoulder. "Before you go, tell me your name."

"Rose Flint," said Rose, without thinking.

"And, pardner, you can call me Alkali Jones," said Alkali, touching the tip of his cowboy hat.

"We're the Treasure Hounds," said Stanley proudly. "Maybe you've heard of us?"

"Treasure Hounds," he said. He looked down at the copy of the hieroglyphics and smiled. "I see. Ah, yes, I see."

"Well," said Rose. She took a deep breath and stepped backward. "I guess we'd better be going."

"Come back soon," he said. He pointed to the paper and smiled. "And don't forget to bring the rest of the note."

Rose smiled weakly and gave Orion a tiny wave. "See you around."

Then, grabbing Alkali with one hand and Stanley with the other, she spun her friends around, and together they hurried out of the hall and into the warm, starry night.

The Hounds had come to the meeting of the Order of the Sphinx hoping for some answers. But it now appeared that all they'd come away with were more questions.

4

Doctor Gardener

THE HOUNDS AGREED they wouldn't show Mr. Orion any more of the message, at least not for the time being.

"I don't trust him," said Alkali. "I'm sure he didn't tell us the truth about what was really in the note."

"That could be, but what are our choices?" said Stanley. "Who else in town knows ancient Egyptian?"

"Maybe we can figure it out ourselves," suggested Rose. "I bet there are lots of books on hieroglyphics at the library."

As it turned out, there were. In fact, when the Hounds went to the library the next day, they were surprised to discover three shelves filled with books on ancient Egypt.

"Hmmm," said Alkali, examining a work on the building of the pyramids. "No wonder there's so much Egyptian stuff here. Most of these books have been donated by the Shadow Beach Order of the Sphinx."

For the next two hours Alkali, Stanley, and Rose searched through book after book, looking for clues as to what the symbols on the back of the photograph meant. They looked at hundreds of hieroglyphics, including pictures of striped snakes, winged beetles, fancy barges, and even a pair of cats dressed in long robes and golden wigs.

But nothing they saw looked like the writing on the back of the photo. However, inside the cover of a book called *The Founding of the Shadow Beach Order of the Sphinx,* Stanley discovered something nearly as exciting: a picture of a young woman standing on the steps of Sphinx Hall.

"Hey! Look at this," he said. "It's the lady in the locket!"

"Well, I'll be," said Alkali. "That's her, all right."

"'Eloise Gardener, Shadow Beach bank teller and founder of the Order of the Sphinx, at the opening of Sphinx Hall,' " said Rose, reading off the caption beneath the picture.

"No wonder she knew how to write hieroglyphics," said Stanley.

"Gardener, Gardener," said Alkali, stroking his chin. "Isn't there someone else in town with that name?"

"Sure," said Rose. "Doctor Gardener, the dentist."

"Do you think they could be related?" said Alkali. "If so, he might know something about the message."

"We ought to at least investigate," said Rose. "Why don't we give him a call?"

"Sounds like a good idea to me," said Alkali. He pointed to a pay phone near the front desk. "We'll call him from there."

Near the phone there was a phone book. After

looking up the number, Rose read it off as Alkali dialed.

"This could be the break we've been looking for," said Alkali as the phone was ringing. "If—"

"Hello, Doctor Gardener's office. May I help you?" said a woman, answering the phone.

"Yes, my name is Alkali Jones, and I'd like to talk to Doctor Gardener. Is he in?"

"He's going to be with patients for the rest of the day," said the receptionist. "Would you like to make an appointment?"

"Could you tell him it's about an Eloise Gardener. We were wondering if he's related to her. You see, we have a hieroglyphic note she wrote, and we're trying to find out if he knows what it might mean," Alkali explained. "So it's very important that we talk to him."

"Hold on a moment. I'll check with the doctor," said the receptionist.

The receptionist never did return to the phone. But an anxious Doctor Gardener did. "Hello! Hello!" he said in a deep voice. "Is this Alkali Jones?"

"Speaking."

"What's this about some hieroglyphics written by my grandmother?" he asked. "Was this something you found down at the Sphinx club?"

"No, sir," said Alkali. "This was something written on the back of a photo we found in an old locket. We've been trying to translate it, and thought that maybe you might know something about it."

Doctor Gardener lowered his voice. "Her locket!"

he gasped. "Where are you right now? I must see you at once."

"We're at the library," said Alkali.

"Don't move!" he commanded. Then, Alkali heard him address his receptionist, saying, "Cancel all my appointments."

"Doctor, that's really not necessary," said Alkali. "If you wish, we'd be glad to—"

"Don't leave the library!" the doctor ordered, just before hanging up. "I'll be there in five minutes."

Alkali put down the phone and licked at his lips.

"Wow," he said, "I've got a feeling we're on to something big. Really big. Gardener is on his way here this very moment, and he sounded as excited as all get-out." Alkali took off his hat and slapped it against his knee. "Whoooeee," he exclaimed. "I got a feeling these hieroglyphics are going to make us rich."

5

The Mystery Deepens

NOT TEN MINUTES after Alkali got off the phone, Doctor Gregory Gardener, still wearing his white dentist's coat, came bursting into the library. He paused at the door for a moment to catch his breath, then looked about the library till his eyes settled on the Treasure Hounds.

"Doctor Gardener?" said Alkali.

Doctor Gardener squinted through thick glasses and brushed a hand through his thick, wavy black hair.

"Alkali Jones?"

Alkali extended his hand. "Pleased to meet you, pardner." He pointed to Rose and Stanley. "These are my friends, Rose Flint and Stanley Duggins. Together we're the Treasure Hounds."

"Treasure Hounds!" said Doctor Gardener. "Ah ha, now I see."

"Doctor Gardener," said Rose. She handed him the slip of paper she'd earlier shown to Ramses, half the hieroglyphic message. They weren't taking any chances with Gardener either. "I wonder if you might be able to translate this for us? It's the hieroglyphics we found on the back of Eloise Gardener's photo."

"The one that was in the locket," explained Alkali.

Doctor Gardener took the slip of paper, glanced at it briefly, then shook his head. "I can't read this. It's just a bunch of weird drawings as far as I'm concerned." He put his hands on his hips and glared at the Hounds. "On the phone you said you had my grandmother's locket along with her photo. That's what I want."

"I'm sorry, sir," said Rose, "but until we know what the writing on the back of your grandmother's picture says, we just can't give it up."

"I hope you understand," said Alkali.

"No," said Doctor Gardener. "Quite frankly, I don't understand." He paused and shook his head. "My grandmother Eloise was my favorite relative, but all I have of her are my memories. Naturally, when I heard you had a locket and photo, I wanted them for my own."

Rose smiled. "And, Doctor Gardener, you'll have them. That's a promise."

"You mean it?" said the doctor.

"I do," said Rose. "I understand how you must feel. As soon as the message is translated, I promise we'll give you the photo."

"But—but—" stammered Doctor Gardener, "I must have it now." He reached into his back pocket and pulled out his wallet. "How much do you want for it? I'm prepared to pay."

"I'm sorry," said Alkali.

"How about fifty dollars?" said the doctor. He opened his wallet and grabbed a handful of bills.

Stanley's eyes got round as saucers at the sight of all that money, but Rose wasn't impressed.

"When we're done with it, we'll give it to you for free," she said. "Till then—"

"How about a hundred, then?" said the doctor.

"It's not for sale," said Alkali firmly.

"Two hundred dollars," said the doctor desperately. He held out his wallet. "Here, take whatever you want. Just let me have those hieroglyphics."

Rose patted the pocket on her blouse. "They stay right in here—for now."

"I don't understand why you won't sell the photograph," said the doctor. "The writings on it are probably the scribblings of a young woman. Of no importance at all."

"Funny," said Alkali, "that's almost exactly what Ramses Orion said."

"Ramses Orion!" gasped the doctor. "Has he seen the photo?"

"No, no," said Rose quickly. "He saw the same thing you did, half the message."

The doctor looked around hastily. The library was nearly deserted, but nevertheless he lowered his voice to a bare whisper. "Orion must not see that message. Is that clear?"

Alkali scratched the side of his head. "You know, we're beginning to get the idea that your grandmother wrote down something pretty important. Mind telling us what you think her hieroglyphics might mean?"

Doctor Gardener chewed on his lower lip for a moment and thought. Finally, he said, "I already told you I don't know how to read hieroglyphics. All I want is a remembrance of my grandmother."

"I promise you the locket and the photo will be yours at the appropriate time," said Rose. "In the meantime, any help you can give us in solving the mystery will be appreciated."

Doctor Gardener drew in a deep breath. "I'll keep that in mind." He nodded. "Now, if you'll excuse me, I've got to get back to work. I've got a patient with a mouthful of instruments sitting back at the office. I'm afraid I left her in a bit of a hurry."

Rose smiled. "We'll be in touch."

Doctor Gardener pointed a finger at Rose. "And so will I," he said. "Of that you can be sure."

6

Library Surprise

THE THREE HOUNDS SPENT the next two days at the library, trying desperately to decipher the message on the back of Eloise Gardener's photograph.

"Let's face it; it's hopeless," said Alkali near the end of the second day. "It takes people a lifetime to learn hieroglyphics. We've only been at it a couple of days."

"Yeah, but in those couple of days we've already figured out part of the message," said Rose. She turned to Stanley, seated next to her at a long library table covered with books and papers. "What do we have so far?"

Stanley picked up a yellow pad and read off the translated message, "'Friends of Egypt!'"

"Go on," said Rose.

"That's it," said Stanley. "That's all we've got."

Rose drew back her head and wrinkled her brow. "But I thought we had much more. What happened to that stuff about the cats and the moon?"

"You mean the message that said, 'Cute cats wearing wigs and pajamas are munching on the moon'?" Alkali asked.

"Yeah, yeah," said Rose. "What happened to that part?"

"It happened to all be wrong," said Alkali. "I just discovered that Stanley had been looking at the hieroglyphics upside-down."

"Great," moaned Rose. She picked up the photograph and stared into Eloise's eyes. "What is your secret, Mrs. Gardener? Oh, how I wish you could speak."

Alkali reached over and took the photograph between his fingers.

"Unfortunately, dead people can't speak, and neither can their pictures," he said. He tossed the picture onto the table with disgust. "Let's face it, pardners. We're wasting our time."

Stanley sighed and set down his yellow pad. "I hate to admit it, but Alkali's right. We're getting nowhere fast."

"So what do you suggest?" said Rose. "Give up?"

"No, but I do suggest we give up trying to break the code ourselves," said Alkali. He bent down and gathered up the books before him. "It's late. Let's put all this stuff back on the shelves. Tomorrow we can start working on another plan."

"Another plan?" said Stanley, gathering up his own books. "What do you have in mind?"

"I don't know," said Alkali, leading the Hounds into the stacks. "But I'm sure if we put our heads together, we can come up with something."

"What about contacting Orion again?" suggested Rose as she was reshelving a copy of *The Mummy's Secret*. "Maybe we can work out some kind of a deal."

"With that creep?" Stanley sneered. "You got to be kidding. I wouldn't trust that guy for a minute."

"What's wrong?" said Alkali, putting away the last of his books. "Didn't you have fun with him the other night?"

"Fun!" Rose laughed. "I'll say he had fun. Orion had him rolling in the aisles all evening."

Even Stanley couldn't help laughing at Rose's joke. In fact, the three Hounds were still chuckling as they came out of the stacks and headed for their belongings on the table.

"When your parents asked you where you were the other night, did you tell them you were tied up in a meeting?" Alkali laughed.

"Very funny," said Stanley.

"Hey," said Rose, pointing at the library table. "Where's the photograph?"

"Whose?" Stanley asked.

"Whose do you think, Stanley?" said Rose. She turned to Alkali. "Remember? I gave it to you."

Alkali rubbed his chin. "I think I tossed it on the table. In fact, I'm sure I did." Now he studied Rose. "You sure you didn't pick it up?"

"Believe me," said Rose, "I would remember something like that." She desperately searched the table. "Oh, this is terrible! It's gone!"

Alkali raised his hand. "Whoa! No need to panic." He got down on his hands and knees and searched under the table. "Maybe it fell on the floor."

But it was nowhere in sight.

"Maybe it's in the pad," said Stanley, shaking out his yellow notebook.

But nothing fell out.

The Hounds scanned the library quickly, but aside from the librarian, there was no one else in the room.

"It's been stolen," declared Rose. "There's no other reasonable explanation."

"But—but who would want to steal an old lady's picture?" said Stanley. "It doesn't make sense."

Rose rolled her eyes. "Stanley, it wasn't the picture they were after. It was the writing on the back."

"But who?" wondered Stanley.

"Who do you think?" said Alkali. "This is one mystery even an idiot could figure out."

"The librarian?" asked Stanley hesitantly.

"Of course not," said Alkali. "The thief has to be either Ramses Orion or Doctor Gregory Gardener. They're the only ones who know that we're on the trail of a treasure."

"And both of them seemed awfully interested in the hieroglyphics, too," said Rose.

"So where do we start?" asked Alkali. "With the dentist or the mummy maker?"

"If it were up to me, we wouldn't start with either," said Stanley. "Those guys could be dangerous."

Rose glanced at Stanley. "Luckily, it's not up to you," she said. "I suggest we start with Doctor Gardener. He was the last one we saw."

"And he did seem to want that picture awful badly," said Alkali as he glanced up at the clock on the wall. "Five thirty-six. He could have left his office at five, come over here, snatched the photo when our backs were turned, and by now be halfway home."

"Or halfway to the treasure," said Rose. "We can't let him get away with this."

"Maybe we should call the police," said Stanley.

"And tell them what?" said Rose. "We don't have a lick of evidence. Only theories."

The Hounds picked up the rest of their belongings and silently began to walk out of the library, quiet for a moment, with their thoughts.

"I think we ought to go by Doctor Gardener's office. Tomorrow's Saturday. So let's meet early and have a little talk with that sneaky dentist," said Rose. "If he's guilty, it shouldn't be that hard to trip him up."

"But what if he thinks we're going to turn him in?" said Stanley. "No telling what he might do."

"What's wrong?" said Alkali, opening the door out of the library. "Afraid Gardener might drill you?"

"It's not funny," said Stanley. "He could do anything."

The Hounds stepped out into the cool evening air and paused for a moment on the sidewalk. "Visiting him in his office is the safest thing we could do," said Rose. "He wouldn't dare try anything in front of his patients."

"Makes sense," said Alkali. "What time shall we meet there?"

"How about eleven o'clock?" said Rose. "The place should be full by then."

"Let's make our visit short and sweet," said Stanley. "Dentists' offices give me the creeps. Someone's always screaming."

Alkali sighed. "Tomorrow, let's hope those screamers don't turn out to be the Shadow Beach Treasure Hounds."

7

Hot on the Trail

WHEN THE TREASURE HOUNDS showed up at Doctor Gardener's office the next morning, they found the place in an uproar. Kids were running wild. A white-haired man waving a shiny red cane was standing on a chair, screaming something about his teeth. And, near the door to Gardener's private office, a fat man with his hand on his swollen cheek was arguing with the nurse. The nurse, a tall, red-lipped woman with a white cap perched crazily on her head, looked nearly hysterical.

"This tooth is killing me!" The man moaned loudly. "The doctor's got to pull it—and soon."

"I'm sorry, Mr. Cedric," said the nurse, "but—"

"Nurse Adams!" interrupted the white-haired man. He stepped off the chair and came her way, waving his cane. "This delay is outrageous. I'm starving, and until I get my teeth I can't eat!"

Miss Adams stepped back swiftly, just in case the man meant to use the cane. "Mr. Brett," she said, "we're trying our best. Please try to be patient."

"I am being patient," said the toothless Mr. Brett. "It's my stomach that can't wait."

The Hounds exchanged confused glances and fought

their way through the room to where Miss Adams was frantically trying to open a door.

"Excuse me," said Rose, tugging at the woman's white sleeve. "Could you tell me when I might be able to have a word with Doctor Gardener?"

Miss Adams turned around and brushed away Rose's hand. "Please, young lady," she said, "leave me alone. Can't you see I'm trying to get out of this zoo?"

"But all I want to know is where I can find the doctor," said Rose.

Miss Adams turned back to the door and tugged again at the knob. "We'd all like to know what happened to Doctor Gardener, but the man has disappeared. It's as simple as that."

"Here," said Alkali, taking hold of the doorknob, "I think you're just twisting the knob the wrong way." He gave it a turn, and the door swung open. "Tell me, ma'am, why do you say he disappeared?"

"Because that's just what he did," said Miss Adams over her shoulder as she hurried through the open door. "He's not here, and he's not at his house. You figure it out."

Mr. Brett screamed, "My teeth!"

Mr. Cedric moaned, "My tooth!"

Nurse Adams shut her eyes for a moment to collect herself. "If I knew where he was, believe me, I'd tell you. Now, please, let me alone!" And with the words still hanging in the air, she slammed the door.

"Strange," said Rose.

"Funny he'd ignore his patients," said Stanley.

"Nothing funny or strange about it at all," said Alkali. "Gardener is probably so busy hunting up that treasure, he probably plumb forgot he's a dentist." He raised an eyebrow. "Or maybe he's already found the treasure and up and retired. Without telling anyone, of course."

"My teeth!" yelled Mr. Brett, banging on the door with his cane. "Let me in there!"

Rose cast a wary eye at Mr. Brett. He looked so mad, she was afraid he might soon start pounding on more than just the door. "Let's get out of here," she said. "I've never seen so many crazy people in one place."

Stanley and Alkali didn't need further encouragement. With Stanley leading, the Hounds fought their way out of the office.

Outside in the hallway, Alkali said, "Hounds, the way I see it, we have no choice. We have to look up Ramses Orion and find out what he knows about this treasure."

"Ramses Orion!" said Stanley. "What makes you think we can trust him for the truth?"

"I'm not sure we can," said Alkali, "but I don't see where we have a choice. If we offer to go partners with him, we still might be able to beat Gardener to the loot."

"Partners? With that nut?" said Stanley.

"It's that or nothing," said Alkali.

Rose nodded. Alkali was right. They had no choice.

"Orion's house is over on Libby Street," she said. "If we hurry, we can be there in five minutes."

Stanley shook his head. "All right," he said, "but I've got a bad feeling about this."

Alkali laughed. "Stanley, you've had a bad feeling about everything. Now, come on, let's go."

Though the Hounds had never before been to Ramses Orion's house, they knew exactly where it was. For that matter, everyone in town knew where Mr. Orion lived. His house was hard to miss. For one thing it was the only house in Shadow Beach that was painted gold. It was also the only house in town with a ten-foot plastic pyramid on the front lawn.

When the Hounds arrived at Orion's, they were surprised to find the front door standing wide open and no one in sight.

"Oh, Mr. Orion?" said Rose, sticking her head in the doorway. "Yoo-hoo! Anyone home?"

Stanley looked over Rose's shoulder and peered into the front room. To his surprise he didn't see anything Egyptian inside. In fact, it looked very much like his own home. From where he stood, he could make out a blue couch, some straight-backed chairs, a fireplace, and a large painting of a snowcapped mountain.

Rose knocked on the door and called again, but there was no reply.

"I don't get it," said Alkali. "Where could he be?"

Just then the Hounds heard a tremendous clatter, as if a row of garbage cans had been knocked over. Stanley nearly leaped out of his shoes. "What was that?"

Alkali stuck his head in the doorway and peered around. Against one wall he saw a staircase leading down to a basement. "I think it came from downstairs," he said.

Rose took a step into the house, leaned toward the staircase, and called out loudly, "Mr. Orion! Mr. Orion! Are you okay?"

No reply.

"Mr. Orion!" Rose bit her lip as she waited for an answer.

Nothing.

She shook her head, then turned around. "I think we'd better go downstairs and see if Mr. Orion is all right. He could be hurt. That was a terrible noise."

"Terrible is right," said Stanley. "All the more reason to get out of here while we still can. What if there's a mummy down there or something?"

"Stanley, I'm surprised at you," said Rose. "Mr. Orion might be injured. We can't just walk away."

Alkali nodded. "Rose is right." He put his hand on Stanley's elbow and led him into the house. "Come on. This will only take a minute to check out."

The Hounds paused at the top of the basement stairs and peered down. At the bottom of the stairs, there was a golden door, adorned with the picture of a giant cobra. Rose looked at her partners, took a deep breath, and headed slowly down toward the cobra door.

Stanley couldn't get his eyes off the snake. Its piercing red eyes seemed to be looking right through him. "I've got a really bad feeling about this," he murmured to himself.

When they got to the bottom of the stairs, Rose paused, then slowly opened the golden door.

"Do—do you see anything?" asked Stanley, staring into the dimly lit room over Rose's shoulder. "It looks awfully dark in there."

"Mr. Orion?" called Rose. "It's the Treasure Hounds. Are you okay?"

There was no response.

Alkali whistled. "Hey! Anyone there?"

Silence.

"Let's get out of here," said Stanley. He squinted and tried to see into the room. "Who knows what Orion might have lurking about in his basement."

Rose's heart was thumping pretty fast, but she tried her best to act calm. "We've gone this far," she said. "Come on. We can't turn back now."

The three Hounds tiptoed into the room, then paused for a moment till Alkali found the light switch.

"Oh, my!" gasped Rose as she slowly surveyed the room.

"Wow!" said Alkali. "This is incredible. It's like something out of the movies."

"Or out of ancient Egypt!" said Stanley. "I've never seen anything like it."

Against one wall was a giant gold throne, covered with blue hieroglyphics. Thick purple curtains covered another wall, and on another hung a huge oil painting depicting thousands of sweating men dragging blocks of stone across the desert toward a half-finished pyramid. Nearby was a small black table that was bare except for a shallow gold dish filled with some sort of a shimmering liquid.

Alkali leaned over and sniffed the contents of the bowl. "It's incense—some kind of Egyptian oil used to freshen up tombs, no doubt."

Stanley gave Alkali a horrified look. "Tombs?"

Alkali smiled. "Look around, pal. Does this look to you like your average basement? See any Ping-Pong tables, or washers and dryers?"

Stanley shuddered and cast his eyes about the room. When he spotted a pair of mummies, their bandages all frayed and yellow, leaning against a wall, he felt certain Alkali had been right about the purpose of the room. The sight sent a shiver rippling down his spine. "Come on, you guys. Let's scram. It's obvious he's not here."

"In a minute, in a minute," said Rose. "Don't be in such a hurry. We still don't know what made that noise."

Stanley swallowed and glanced back at the stairway. "I'm telling you guys, this place is just like where the scientist ran into that killer monster in *The Mummy's Curse*."

Rose shook her head. "Stanley, please. This is not the movies. It's real life."

"I know," said Stanley. "That's what makes it all the worse."

Rose smiled. "If you're that frightened, then just stay by the stairs. Alkali and I will look around."

Stanley waved them on. "Be my guest."

Just then, something behind Stanley went "ARRRAWAK!" The poor boy leaped nearly a foot into the air. For that matter, so did Alkali and Rose.

"Wha—wha—" stammered Stanley, afraid to turn around.

"What was that?" gasped Alkali.

"A—a bird!" said Rose, spinning about and spying a huge black falcon perched atop a silver stand. The bird tilted his head and eyed the Hounds. "ARRRAWAK!"

Stanley turned around slowly and put his hand on his chest. "I've never been so scared in my life," he said, shaking his head.

"Me neither," said Alkali, gesturing toward the bird. "Wouldn't you know Orion would have something like this for a pet."

"He looks just like some of the hieroglyphics we've been studying," said Rose. She took a deep breath and glanced into the shadows near the throne. "Come on, we've got to finish our search. You still staying here, Stanley?"

Stanley looked at the throne, then back at the bird. "I'm sticking with you two, thanks. Come on, let's make this quick."

The Hounds quickly crossed the room and began poking about in the shadows, looking for whatever it was that had made the clatter they'd heard earlier. They discovered a worn wooden desk covered with papers and books and stacks of bandages similar to those Orion had used to tie up Stanley. Then they discovered what had made the racket. In the corner lay three small trash cans that had been filled with all kinds of nails, nuts, and bolts, but were now empty, their contents having been spilled onto the floor.

"So this is what must have made that noise," said Rose, bending over and picking up a large, rusty bolt. "But what could have tipped them over?" She looked over at the pair of mummies against the far wall. "If only mummies could talk," she said, "what secrets they could tell."

"I'm not sure I want a mummy whispering in my ear," said Stanley. He sat down on the pile of bandages, reached out, and began picking through the scattered contents of the cans. "Frankly, I'd prefer that these old Egyptians keep their secrets to themselves."

"But, Stanley, don't you want to know how these cans fell down?" asked Rose.

"If you ask me, they just tipped over on their own," said Stanley. "Ouch!" He turned and looked back at Alkali. "Stop it, will you?"

Alkali tilted his head and furrowed his brow. "What are you talking about?"

Stanley rolled his eyes toward the ceiling. "Come on, Alkali, you know exactly what I'm talking about."

Alkali laughed. "No, I don't."

Stanley wagged a finger in Alkali's face. "Don't try to tell me you didn't just kick me, Alkali Jones, because I know it wasn't Rose."

Alkali raised his hand. "Pardner, I swear I didn't touch you."

Stanley's eyes suddenly got round as saucers. He gulped, then shot to his feet, propelled by another kick, this one even stronger.

"The bandages!" yelled Rose, backing away. "They're moving!"

"I've got news for you," said Alkali, backing across the room. "That's not just a pile of bandages. It's— it's—"

As they watched in horror, the pile of rags began rolling their way.

"Oh, no!" screamed Stanley. "Run for your lives! It's a mummy!"

8

The Talking Mummy

THE HOUNDS SCRAMBLED out of the basement and up the stairs as if a fire were licking at their heels. They hit the landing at a run, dashed out the door, and didn't stop till they were safely outside on the sidewalk.

"I wouldn't have believed it if I hadn't seen it with my own two eyes," said Alkali, bent over at the waist, gasping for breath. "Wow! A living, breathing mummy!"

"It sure wasn't Orion's dirty laundry," said Stanley. He kept one eye on the open door, just in case the monster suddenly came tumbling out. "I hope you guys believe me now. You see, mummies can walk."

"That mummy didn't walk; it rolled," said Rose. "Anyway, I'm not so sure that thing was real."

Stanley looked at his partner as if she had lost her senses. "What are you talking about? Didn't you just see it try to attack us?"

"I noticed you running pretty fast, Rose Flint," said Alkali. "Come on, now, you were just as scared as we were."

"I'll admit my emotions may have gotten the better of me for a moment," said Rose. "But now that I've had a chance to think over everything logically . . ."

"What does logic have to do with it?" Stanley put his freckled nose in Rose's face. "Don't try to tell me that wasn't a mummy. It was! Plain as day."

Rose glanced back at the house. "A mummy on the outside, perhaps, but underneath—a live person."

"What?" said Alkali.

"Think about it," said Rose. "Mummies can't move. They're dead. Only someone alive could have kicked Stanley. I'm telling you, guys, someone's in trouble down there—maybe even Ramses Orion."

Alkali nodded. "Hmmm, could be, I suppose."

"Only one way to find out," said Rose. She motioned toward the door.

Stanley put up his hands and began backing away. "Oh, no. You're not getting me back inside there. No way."

"I don't know," said Alkali.

Rose started back up the walkway toward the front door. "Chickens," she said.

"Rose," said Stanley, "please don't be a fool."

Rose paused at the door. "Look," she said, "I thought the Hounds were supposed to stick together. Do you want to share this treasure or not?"

Alkali licked at his lips. There was almost nothing he wouldn't do for treasure. "You mean if it is Ramses in there, you're not going to tell us what he has to say?"

"Are we a team or not?" said Rose.

Alkali sighed and started up the walkway. "Come on, Stanley. She's right. We got in this together, we've got to finish it up the same way."

"But—but," stammered Stanley, "the mummy!"

"Stanley, he's just a pile of rags. He can't even walk," said Rose. "Come. He may need our help."

Stanley shook his head. "This treasure better be worth it," he said, heading for the door. He took a deep breath before stepping inside. "This, my friends, is the stupidest thing we've ever done."

With that, the Hounds edged their way back down the stairs. Pausing at the bottom, Rose craned her neck into the room till she spotted the mummy, still rolling about on the floor.

"Hello?" she called cautiously. "Do you need help?"

The mummy replied by breathing heavily and bouncing up and down, just as Stanley had a few days earlier on the table at Sphinx Hall.

"Stay where you are," said Rose. She stepped gingerly into the room. "We're here to help."

With Rose in the lead, the Hounds made their way to where the mummy lay thrashing about on the floor. It reminded Rose of a crazy man in a straitjacket. "We're going to get you out of those bandages," she said, kneeling down beside the mummy and touching its head. "Please, try not to move."

Instantly, the mummy stopped moving and lay perfectly still.

"See," said Rose, looking up at her friends, who were standing above her, wide eyed as owls. "He understands."

"Rose, be careful," said Stanley. "In *The Mummy's Curse,* this is exactly how the creature got loose. A scientist unwrapped him just like you're doing now. Then the thing—"

"Stanley, would you please be quiet," said Rose, without looking up. "This happens to be a very delicate operation I'm about to perform."

After untying a knot at the side of the mummy's head, Rose slowly began to unwrap the bandages, certain that she would soon be looking into the eyes of Ramses Orion. On the other hand, Alkali had no idea what to expect, while Stanley was convinced they'd be staring at the hollow eyes and wrinkled face of a three-thousand-year-old Egyptian.

But the first thing that came into view was a pile of black, wavy hair, then a pair of thick glasses.

"Oh, my!" said Rose.

"It's Doctor Gardener!" exclaimed Alkali.

"What are you doing here?" Stanley gasped.

"Ummm, ummm, ugh," mumbled the doctor, his mouth still covered by the bandages.

Alkali bent down and quickly removed the last of the bandages from the doctor's face.

"Oh, thank heavens you found me," said Doctor Gardener the moment he could speak. "If you hadn't come along when you did, I think I would have been a goner."

"How did you get in this mess, anyhow?" asked Rose.

"How do you think?" said the doctor. "Orion did it. I came by this morning to find out what he knew about my grandmother's photo. To my surprise I found him down here, examining it under a magnifying

glass." Gardener glared up at Rose. "I thought you said you weren't going to give it to him."

"I didn't," said Rose. She looked at the Hounds and nodded. "He must have stolen it last night at the library."

Doctor Gardener raised his head and stared down at his bound body. "Please, could you get the rest of this stuff off me. If Orion finds us here, we'll all be mummies—permanently."

Stanley gulped and looked back at the door. "Hurry up," he said. "I've already been a mummy once, and believe me, I have no interest in reliving the experience."

"When I heard you upstairs, I knocked over those cans," said Doctor Gardener. "I was hoping you'd come down to investigate."

"I'm glad we did," said Rose, as she and Alkali worked quickly, unwrapping the bandages by rolling the doctor across the floor like a log. "Do you have any idea where Orion might be right now?"

BANG! The sudden sound of a slamming door froze everyone in place for a moment.

"Uh, oh," whispered Alkali. "I've got a horrible feeling your question about the whereabouts of Mr. Orion has just been answered."

Stanley glanced up at the ceiling and listened to the sounds of footsteps crossing the living room.

"We've got to get out of here!" he whispered.

"No time for that now," said Gardener. His mind was working lickety-split. "Quick—wrap me up again and roll me back to where you found me. Then hide. If Orion comes down here and finds me missing, he'll tear this place apart."

Rose looked about the room desperately.

"Just do as I say," ordered the doctor. "Orion is too dangerous to fool with, especially now that the treasure is within his grasp."

"Treasure!" said Alkali. "So I was right. What kind of a treasure?"

"Wrap me up. Hurry," said Doctor Gardener. "We can talk about the treasure later—if we get out of this."

Stanley gulped. "If—if!" he moaned.

"Hurry! There may not be much time," said the doctor.

The three Hounds knelt down and rolled Doctor Gardener quickly across the floor, as they would wrap up a rug. When they were done, the dentist was once more a mummy, lying against the wall.

Suddenly the sounds of footsteps came echoing down the stairs.

"Here he comes!" whispered Rose.

"And here we go!" said Alkali. He turned off the light and then grabbed his partners and scooted across the room, ducking behind the giant gold throne just as Ramses Orion started down the basement stairs.

Alkali peeked out and saw Orion enter the room and turn on the light. Dressed as usual in his golden robe, he walked over and took the big black falcon off its perch and placed it on his wrist.

"Hello, Cleopatra. Surprised to see me back so soon?" He strode across the floor to his desk. "Can you imagine, Cleopatra, I left here in such a hurry I forgot to copy the translation."

After placing the bird on the corner of the desk, he turned to the twitching form of Doctor Gregory

Gardener. "Save your strength, my friend. You're never going to get free. Never!" And he let out an awful laugh that sent chills rolling up the spines of the Treasure Hounds.

No doubt about it, thought Alkali, Orion is one dangerous dude.

As the Hounds watched, Orion picked up a pencil and a pad of paper and began frantically writing. When he had finished, he ripped a sheet from the pad and held it aloft. "At last! A guide to the greatest treasure in the history of Shadow Beach." He kissed the paper and gave Cleopatra a pat. "Perhaps, my sweet, a guide to the greatest treasure ever!"

Spinning about on his heels, he walked quickly over to the black table and dipped his fingers into the shallow gold bowl. "May the oil of life guide me to the riches!" he said. He drew out his hand and rubbed the oil between his fingers. "And may the oil also guide the Treasure Hounds"—he cackled madly—"guide them to their doom!"

The Hounds shrunk back behind the throne and exchanged looks of horror. "Do you think that stuff really works?" whispered Stanley.

"We'd better hope not," Rose whispered back. "Know what I mean?"

Stanley gulped and nodded. He knew exactly what she meant.

"Cleopatra!" cried Ramses. "Soon we'll be on our way to Egypt, just you and me, with enough money to live the way we deserve. Like my great ancestor, King Tut himself!"

The Hounds peeked out from behind the throne just in time to see Orion return Cleopatra to her perch.

"Sounds like Orion has a few screws loose," whispered Alkali.

"A few!" Rose whispered back. "This guy is a candidate for the loony bin."

Orion gave Cleopatra one last pat, then rubbed his hands together gleefully. "At last, my fine-feathered friend, the treasure is within our reach." He pointed to the door. "Onward! Fortune awaits!"

Slamming the door behind him, he disappeared into the stairwell. A few moments later the Hounds heard the front door close, and the house fell silent.

"Wow," said Alkali, as soon as he was sure Orion was gone, "that was close."

"Too close," said Stanley. He stood up and glanced about the room nervously. "Come on, let's unwind Doctor Gardener and get out of here before that wacko returns."

"Alkali, help Stanley with Doctor Gardener," said Rose. She crossed quickly to Orion's desk. "I'll see if I can't find the hieroglyphic translation. If so, maybe we can beat him to the treasure."

It wasn't long before Alkali and Stanley had freed the doctor.

"Rose, come on," said Stanley, helping the dentist to his feet. "We may not have much time."

Rose shuffled through the papers hastily. "I'll be there in a minute," she said.

"Take your time," said Alkali. He was standing at the door, his hand on the knob. "I think we're going to be here a while."

"What?" gasped Stanley.

"The door," said Alkali, tugging on it with all his might. "It's stuck. I can't budge it an inch."

9

Treasure Bound

ALKALI PULLED ON THE DOOR till his face grew red. Then he kicked at it till his foot hurt. All the while Stanley stood right behind him, cheering him on. But neither Alkali's strength nor Stanley's encouragement budged the door an inch.

"Is it locked?" asked Doctor Gardener.

"Nope, just stuck," said Alkali. "It's jammed in tighter than anything."

"We've got to find a way to loosen it up," said the doctor. "I sure don't want to be here when Orion returns."

"You and I both," said Stanley. He cast his eyes about the room. "Maybe we can find an ax and knock it down."

While Stanley, Alkali, and Doctor Gardener tugged at the door, Rose busied herself at Orion's desk. Hurriedly riffling through the papers, she searched frantically for a clue to the meaning of the hieroglyphics.

"Any luck?" called Alkali.

"None," said Rose, studying a page full of blue and red symbols. "How about you?"

"Nope," said Alkali. His forehead was covered

with sweat. "This thing just won't give."

Doctor Gardener sighed. "I hate to admit it, folks, but this place is starting to look more and more like a tomb every second."

Stanley felt a sudden chill. "We're done for," he moaned. "Orion asked that Egyptian oil to guide us to doom, and it looks like that's exactly what it's doing!"

"Oil!" said Alkali, suddenly letting go of the door. "Of course!"

"Of course is right," said Stanley. "That's a powerful spell he put on us."

Alkali rolled his eyes. "I'm not talking about his dumb spell," said Alkali. "I'm talking about his Egyptian oil. It's just what we need to grease the door." He licked his lips and pointed to the pile of bandages that had earlier bound the doctor. "Put some of those in the oil and bring them over, double quick."

While Stanley scratched at his head, Doctor Gardener gathered up some bandages and dropped them into the dish of Egyptian oil. As soon as they were soaked through, he gave them to Alkali, who quickly ran them along the edge of the door.

"Let's hope this oil seeps into the crack," said Alkali.

"I still don't get it," said Stanley.

"You'll see," said Alkali. He threw down the rags and dried his hands on his pants. "Stand back, everybody."

Stanley and the doctor took a step backward, and Alkali took hold of the door handle. Drawing in a deep breath, he braced a foot against the wall and started to pull.

"Come on, Alkali!" said Stanley.

"Pull!" said the doctor.

"You can do it!" cried Rose.

"Ugh!" groaned Alkali.

The door shivered and creaked, but wouldn't give.

"We need to work together on this," said the doctor. He put his arms around Alkali's waist. Then Stanley grabbed hold of him. Then, all together, they pulled.

"It's opening!" yelled Alkali. "Keep it up."

Greased like a skillet, the door shot open like a bullet from a gun, sending Alkali, Stanley, and the doctor sprawling across the floor.

"We did it!" cried Stanley, getting to his feet. "All right!"

"Let's get out of here," said the doctor, dusting himself off. "If we hurry, maybe we can still find Orion."

"Not so fast," said Rose. "I don't have the translation yet."

"Forget that stupid translation," said Stanley. He waved to Rose. "We've got to get out of here before Orion comes back and rubs us out. Know what I mean?"

Rose's mouth dropped open. "Stanley! That's it!"

"Huh?" said Stanley.

"Rub out! That's how I can get the translation." Rose clapped her palm on her forehead. "Why didn't I think of it before? I swear, Stanley, you're a genius!"

"Confound it, Rose! What are you talking about?" asked Alkali.

Rose picked up the pad of paper Orion had earlier been writing on and waved it at Alkali. "How could

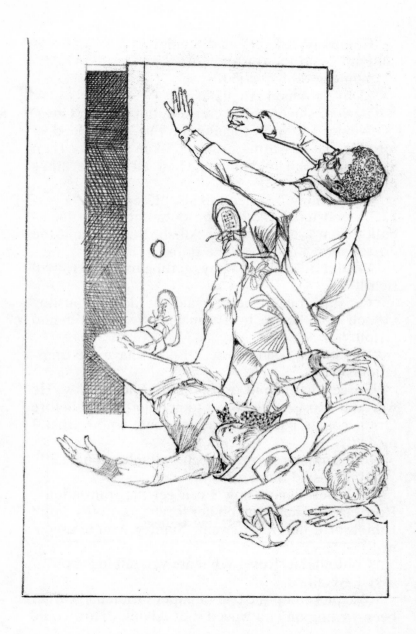

I have been so stupid? The message has been here all along."

Alkali tilted his head. "Rose, have you gone loco? That paper is blank. There's nothing on it."

"Blank?" Rose laughed. She picked up a pencil and held it before her eyes. "See this magic wand? It's going to be our ticket to riches. Just watch."

Alkali, Stanley, and the doctor gathered around and watched, while Rose lightly ran the pencil over the paper.

"I've done that before!" said Stanley. "When I was a kid, I'd put a penny under a piece of paper and shade over it until the penny appeared."

"Well, this is the same principle," Rose explained. "When Orion wrote on the pad, the words were indented on the next page. Now all I have to do is shade it carefully and those words should appear."

Sure enough, just as Rose had predicted, a message soon came into view.

"Listen to this," she said, setting down the pencil. "This is what Orion wrote." Rose read aloud:

> **Friends of Egypt!**
> **At old Sphinx Hall begin the quest**
> **By reading the numbers where the ancients rest.**
> **March off the numbers from that spot,**
> **Straight through the door till you reach the lot.**
> **Then with a shovel start digging down,**
> **And golden coins will soon be found.**

"What did I tell you! It is a treasure map!" exclaimed Alkali.

"I never realized Grandmother was such a fine poet," said Doctor Gardener, smiling.

"Well, I'm not sure it's the greatest poem I've ever read," said Rose, "but it certainly is one of the most exciting."

Stanley raised his eyebrows. "How many gold coins do you think she might have hidden? A lot?"

"Only one way to find out," said Rose. "Follow the directions, dig 'em up, and count them ourselves."

"We have to hurry," said Doctor Gardener. "If the treasure is found, the shame would be terrible."

"Shame?" said Rose. "What shame?"

"Ummm—ahhh—nothing," said Gardener nervously. "Ummm, I meant it would be a shame if Ramses Orion found the coins instead of us."

Stanley glanced nervously up the stairs. "Don't you think we ought to get going? Orion could show up any minute."

"I'm with Stanley," said Doctor Gardener. "Let's get over to Sphinx Hall."

"Sphinx Hall?" said Stanley. Just the mention of the place sent a chill up his spine. "Do we have to go there?"

Rose held Eloise's poem at arm's length and recited the opening lines: "'At old Sphinx Hall begin the quest/By reading the numbers where the ancients rest.'" She lowered the paper and smiled at Stanley. "Sorry, but there's no way around it. Sphinx Hall is our first stop."

"There's not a minute to waste," said Doctor Gardener. He pointed up the stairs. "Let's go. If we hurry, we can be there in ten minutes."

With Doctor Gardener leading the way, the Hounds scrambled up the stairs and out of the house. Outside, they paused for only a moment before striking out toward Sphinx Hall.

"Step lively, now," said Doctor Gardener, urging them on with a wave of his hand. "We're the only ones who can stop Orion from getting his greedy mitts on that gold."

The doctor was in such a hurry that he jogged the entire ten blocks to the hall. It was all the Hounds could do just to keep up. When they got to Sphinx Hall, they collapsed on the steps.

"Up! Up!" said Gardener, standing above them, urging them to their feet. "No time to waste!"

"But, Doctor Gardener," said Alkali, struggling to catch his breath, "can't we just rest for a minute?"

"A minute could be the difference between success and failure!" said Gardener. He pointed toward the hall's big gold door. "For all we know, Orion could be in there right now. I'm telling you that madman has got to be stopped."

The Hounds slowly got to their feet and made their way up the steps. "Are you sure we ought to burst in there?" said Stanley. "What if Orion is inside? A guy with his powers isn't likely to let a couple of kids get in his way."

"What are you talking about? It's four to one," said Gardener. He put his arm on Stanley's shoulder and pulled him through the door. "Believe me, it wouldn't be a fair fight."

He's right, thought Stanley. It wouldn't be a fair fight. Four kids and a crazy dentist against a guy who knows all the ancient Egyptian spells. He shut his eyes and took a deep breath. He figured it was going to take a miracle to get them out of there alive.

10

The Dentist's Secret

AN OLD, OLD MAN, his face so rough and wrinkled he looked as if he'd been mummified, was sitting behind a desk just inside the door of Sphinx Hall.

"Welcome," he said in a shaking voice. "My name is Abner Peale, and I'm Guardian of the House of the Sphinx. Tell me, friends, have you come to seek the ancient truths?"

Doctor Gardener smiled and placed his hands on the desk. "Actually, sir, we're here to seek the resting place of the ancients. Know where that might be?"

"I might," he said.

Doctor Gardener leaned across the desk. "Has Ramses Orion been here today, by chance?"

"Perhaps," said Mr. Peale.

"Is he here now?" asked Stanley.

"Nope, come and gone," said the old man. He narrowed his pale blue eyes and looked over Doctor Gardener and the Hounds. "Weren't you kids here the other night?"

"Yes, sir," said Rose. She pointed to Stanley. "Maybe you remember him. Ramses Orion turned him into a dummy—I mean mummy."

Mr. Peale nodded. "I thought I'd seen you before."
He looked up at the doctor. "And who might you
be?"

"Doctor Gregory Gardener," he replied. "I'm a
dentist here in town and a descendant of Eloise Gardener."

The old man smiled and leaned back in his chair.
"So you're Eloise's grandson," he said. "Your grandmother was quite a woman, young man. I knew her
well. Without her, this organization wouldn't be here
today. She would have done anything for the order.
Anything."

The doctor smiled.

"Too bad about all that unpleasantness at the
bank," he said. "That caused quite a stir around here,
as you might imagine."

Doctor Gardener blushed. "I–I didn't realize there
was anyone who still remembered it," he stammered.

"I'll never forget it." Old man Peale laughed.
"Your grandmother, yes indeed, she was something,
all right."

Doctor Gardener looked around the room to make
sure they weren't being overheard. "Listen, as a favor
to my grandmother's memory, could you tell us where
we might find this resting place of the ancients?"

Mr. Peale smiled. "I guess it wouldn't hurt." He
swiveled about in his chair and pointed to a silver
door in the shape of a giant beetle. "It's right through
there. You can't miss it."

"Thank you," said Doctor Gardener. He turned
back and was about to step away when Abner Peale
suddenly called him back. "One more thing," he said

in that shaking voice of his. "That money your grand-mother stole. It ever turn up?"

Doctor Gardener gulped, then shook his head. "Ummm, money. My grandmother?"

"Stole?" said Rose. She furrowed her brow. "What's this about stolen money?"

"Ummm, ahhh—" stammered Doctor Gardener. "It's nothing, really, nothing."

"Nothing, is it? Gardener, give Eloise her due!" said Mr. Peale. He winked at Rose and leaned forward. "Nearly forty years ago, it is rumored that his grandmother embezzled hundreds of gold coins from the Shadow Beach Savings Bank. Far as I know, the loot has never turned up."

Doctor Gardener put a finger to his lips. "Shhh!" he said. "Please respect my grandmother's memory."

Rose folded her arms across her chest. "Doctor Gardener, I believe you owe us an explanation."

"You certainly do," said Alkali. "The Hounds and I have a right to know what kind of a treasure we're looking for. We want to know the truth, sir. Have the coins been stolen?"

Doctor Gardener sighed. "All right, I'll admit I haven't been totally truthful," he said. "But it was for a good cause."

"It better have been," said Alkali. "We don't like being hoodwinked."

"All I wanted to do was protect my grandmother's reputation," said Doctor Gardener. "She was a wonderful woman and did many fine things in this town, but—"

"But what?" demanded Rose.

"But she got carried away when it came to the Sphinx club. She loved it so much that she wanted to send all its members to Egypt, an impossibility, of course, on a bank teller's salary." He paused and shook his head. "So, in a moment of weakness, she pocketed some gold coins from the bank. Naturally, the theft was soon discovered, and my grandmother was accused."

"Did she go to jail?" asked Stanley.

"Alas, she died before the trial," said Doctor Gardener. "But since the coins were never found, her guilt has always been in doubt. If those coins turn up where her map says they are, then Eloise's name will be forever associated with crime, never with her many good works."

"So if you have your way, those gold coins will never be found," said Rose. "Is that right?"

"Yes, that's why I wanted to buy the photograph and the map—so that the treasure, along with the blot on my grandmother's reputation, would remain buried forever."

"Also being the grandson of a crook wouldn't be too good for business, huh, Doctor?" said Alkali.

Gardener lowered his eyes. "I admit my reasons for wanting to keep this quiet haven't been entirely unselfish," he said.

"I'm sorry," said Alkali, "but we're still going after the treasure. Don't forget. We're not called the Treasure Hounds for nothing."

"We've got a reputation, too," said Rose.

Doctor Gardener sighed. "I guess there's no stopping this thing now. It's already gone too far." He pointed to the giant silver door, the one shaped like a beetle. "Come on, kids, if nothing else, we can still keep that treasure out of the hands of Ramses Orion."

"I'm all for that," said Alkali, "Especially if it means putting it in our hands instead."

On the other side of the silver door, Gardener and the Hounds found themselves in a long narrow room, filled from wall to wall with a huge wooden barge. Covered with strange hieroglyphics, it was at least forty feet long. Rows of oars extended from the sides, and a small mast, bearing a pyramid-shaped sail, rose from the center.

"I thought I'd seen some weird things in my day," whispered Stanley, "but this setup takes the cake."

"'Resting Place of the Ancients,'" said Alkali, reading the words off a brass plaque affixed to the boat's stern. "'May You Encounter Calm Seas and Warm Winds on Your Journey to the Other World.'"

"It's a funeral barge," said Doctor Gardener. "The spirits of the departed are supposed to ride it to the next world."

"Spirits?" said Stanley. "You mean this thing is filled with ghosts?" He looked over his shoulder at the exit. "Ummm, are we just about done?"

"According to Eloise's poem, we're supposed to march off the numbers we find on the ancients' resting spot," said Rose. "March them straight out the door till we reach the lot."

"Numbers?" said Alkali. He bent down and examined the plaque closely. "Numbers! I see them," he exclaimed. "Listen to this: 'Generous gift of Eloise

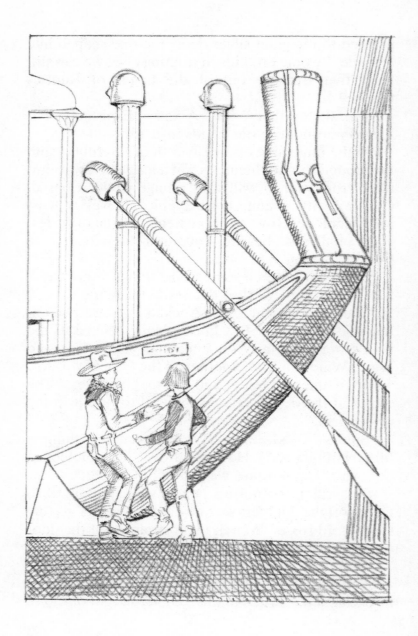

Gardener, 1951.'"

"Nineteen fifty-one," said Rose. "Those must be the numbers we've got to march off."

"They have to be," said Alkali.

Dr. Gardener wheeled about like a soldier, faced the open door, and raised his arm. "Hounds! Attention! Ready to march off one thousand nine hundred and fifty-one steps."

"Ready," said Rose.

Alkali saluted and fell in behind Doctor Gardener. "Ready to march for treasure, sir."

"Those coins are waiting," said Rose.

"Yeah," said Stanley. "And probably so is Ramses Orion. I've got a feeling that nut won't give up those coins without a fight."

11

Fine Fabrics and
Fine Fixes

WITH GARDENER COUNTING OFF THE STEPS, the
Hounds followed him out of the room. As they passed
through the lobby, Abner Peale, the old man at the
desk, called to them in a shaking voice, "Gardener,
wait a minute. I need to—"

"Thirteen, fourteen, fifteen," said Doctor Gardener, dismissing the old man with a wave of his
hand.

"But wait. I've got—"

"Shhh!" said Rose, putting a finger to her lips.
"Don't bother him now. The count must be exact."

Mr. Peale rose unsteadily to his feet and raised his
arm just as the tiny parade was passing through the
front door.

"Gardener! Gardener! Come back here, you—"
But before he could complete his sentence, the door
to the hall slammed, and the treasure hunters marched
off, intent on making sure every step of the way was
counted.

Down the steps of Sphinx Hall and across the street

they went, in single file, till they came to their first obstacle, the Magic Clippers Barber Shop.

"March on through," said Rose, holding the door open. "That's what the poem said to do."

"We have no choice," said Alkali. "When Eloise wrote out her directions, this was all open land. No matter what gets in our way we have to keep going straight."

The barber, Mr. Kurtz, was busy cutting the hair of a grim-faced man with a puffy red nose when the parade came through.

"Forty-seven, forty-eight, forty-nine," said Dr. Gardener.

Mr. Kurtz looked up, astonished.

"See you later," said Rose, waving to the barber as she passed by.

"Hey! Wait a minute!" said Mr. Kurtz as the Hounds filed out his back door. "What's going on?"

"That's what I want to know!" said the man seated in the barber's chair. "Nincompoop! You just snipped off half my hair."

"Whoops," said Mr. Kurtz.

"Sixty-one, sixty-two, sixty-three," said Gardener, leading the Hounds across an alley, through an open gate, and into Mrs. Englander's back yard.

"Why, Doctor Gardener, what a pleasant surprise," said Mrs. Englander, looking up from the bed of pansies she'd been weeding. "To what do I owe this visit?"

"Eighty-eight, eighty-nine, ninety," replied Doctor Gardener.

Mrs. Englander tilted her head. "That's strange,"

she said. "Those were the exact words Ramses Orion spoke when he came through."

"Ramses Orion!" said Stanley, pausing beside Mrs. Englander. "When was he here?"

Mrs. Englander brushed the dirt from her hands and thought. "It couldn't have been more than ten minutes ago, at the most."

"Did you hear that?" shouted Stanley. "Orion is only ten minutes ahead of us."

"Faster," said Rose, and Doctor Gardener picked up the pace. Passing out of Mrs. Englander's yard, they crossed Legion Street, cut through the Abel Lumberyard, and entered the Dobbs Family Day Care Center.

"Look!" said a little boy with strawberry jam smeared across both cheeks. "It's a parade!"

"May I help you?" asked Mrs. Dobbs, smiling.

"Perhaps," said Rose. "Have you seen a man in a long gold robe come through here recently?"

"I sure did," said Mrs. Dobbs. "The kids went absolutely crazy when he marched in a few minutes ago. They thought he was a clown, come to visit."

"Thanks for the information," Alkali called as they passed out the back door.

"Hey! Wait! What's going on?" shouted Mrs. Dobbs.

"Come back!" cried all the children.

"Six hundred and forty-one, six hundred and forty-two," said Doctor Gardener.

As fast as they moved, they couldn't seem to catch up with Orion. But Dan at Foster's Jewelry Shop and Lorraine at Sweet Lor's Candies both said they had missed him by only minutes.

"He can't be far ahead of us now," said Alkali as they stepped through the door of Norman's Fine Fabrics.

"Ah! Doctor Gardener," said Mr. Norman, plastering a big fake smile across his face. "What can I do for you today?"

"Sixteen hundred and nine, sixteen hundred and ten," he replied.

Mr. Norman's eye's lit up. "Sixteen hundred and ten! Is that how many yards of fabric you'd like to buy? Wonderful! What kind of material do you want?"

Alkali patted Mr. Norman on the shoulder as he passed by. "The doc wants to think about it for a while if that's okay with you," he said as the marchers headed into the back storeroom. "We'll come through again later."

"Sixteen hundred and fifteen, sixteen hundred and sixteen," said Doctor Gardener, making his way through Mr. Norman's large storeroom.

"Wow," said Rose, looking at all the multicolored rolls of material stacked along the walls of the deserted storeroom, "I never realized Mr. Norman carried so much fabric."

"Look at all that silk up on the top shelf," said Stanley. "I bet that stuff is worth a fortune."

"Sixteen hundred and thirty," said Doctor Gardener. "Sixteen hundred and— Whoa! Ah! Help!"

"Doctor Gardener!" exclaimed Rose, glancing up just as Doctor Gardener disappeared under a swirl of polka-dotted cotton cloth. But before she had a

chance to react, Ramses Orion appeared from behind the billowing sheet and flung the material over all of their heads, like a fisherman tossing his net.

"Oh, no!" screamed Stanley.

"Help!" cried Rose.

"Glup, gla—" muttered Alkali, before the cotton cloth being tightened around his mouth stilled his voice.

In the wink of an eye, Ramses Orion wrapped up the four of them in one giant roll, tighter than four caterpillars squeezed into a single cocoon.

"Thought you'd beat me to the gold, did you?" Orion laughed at the huge, wriggling bundle. "Surprise! By the time you get to the hiding spot, all you're going to find is an empty hole."

The bundle squirmed in reply.

"So long," said Orion. "Hope I don't see you later."

The last thing they heard was Orion's counting as he marched out the back door on his way to find the buried coins.

For the next few minutes, Doctor Gardener and the Hounds thrashed about the floor in their giant straitjacket, kicking, wriggling, turning, and tossing. But no matter what they did, they couldn't break free, nor could they cry for help. No doubt about it, Ramses Orion knew how to make a mummy.

This is horrible, thought Stanley. The Hounds have been turned into mummies, and Ramses Orion is on his way to the treasure. What a disaster!

What a disaster, thought Doctor Gardener. Those coins will soon see the light of day, along with my grandmother's ruined reputation.

"Look at this room, will you?" The mournful voice of Mr. Norman interrupted their thoughts. "Material is scattered everywhere. It's a disaster area!"

"What happened?" It was a shaky voice. Rose thought she recognized it as belonging to Abner Peale from Sphinx Hall.

"Gardener and those kids must have done it," screamed Mr. Norman. "If they don't come back and clean this up, I'm calling the police."

Please do, thought Stanley. Anything to get out of here.

As it turned out, everyone had the same thought. Desperate to get Mr. Norman's attention, the Hounds and Dr. Gardener started twisting and turning about in the cloth till they made themselves look like a giant jumping bean.

"Great Scott!" said Mr. Norman. "That bolt of cotton—it's alive!"

"Glumpa, glotz!" cried Stanley with all his strength.

"It talks!" said Mr. Peale.

"I'm getting to the bottom of this," said Mr. Norman. "Stand back, Peale!"

A few moments later the Hounds felt the cloth begin to loosen. Then, suddenly, they found themselves tumbling onto the floor as Mr. Norman unraveled the big cotton sheet.

"Ah, ha!" said Mr. Norman. "I thought someone might have been hiding in there."

"Hiding?" said Mr. Peale. "Looks more like someone was trying to mummify them."

"Yeah, guess who?" said Alkali.

"Must have been Ramses Orion," said Mr. Peale. He offered Alkali his hand and helped him up. "No one but Orion can wrap a body that tight."

Doctor Gardener, Rose, and Stanley slowly struggled to their feet. "I'm getting to be a real expert at playing mummy," said Stanley. "Orion has gotten me twice now."

"Me, too," said Doctor Gardener. He shook his finger. "Someday I'd like to get Ramses Orion in my dentist's chair. Then he'd find out—" Gardener suddenly paused in midsentence and slapped his forehead. "Orion! He's on his way to the treasure! What are we doing just standing around?"

Abner Peale raised a shaking hand. "Wait," he said. "Don't go off yet."

Now Gardener raised his hand too. "No time to wait," said the doctor. "Time is running out!"

"But Doctor Gardener," cried Mr. Peale, "I've come all this way so that—"

"Sixteen hundred and thirty-one, sixteen hundred and thirty-two," Doctor Gardener said, taking up the count where he'd left it off fifteen minutes earlier.

"What in the world is going on here?" asked Mr. Norman, scratching the side of his head.

"Tell you later," Alkali called, falling in behind Doctor Gardener.

"We're trying to stop that mad mummy maker," said Rose.

"And save Eloise Gardener's reputation," said Stanley.

Mr. Norman scratched his head some more. "As I said, what in the world is going on?"

12

A Reward From the Past

"NO TIME TO WASTE NOW," said Rose as they were leaving Norman's Fine Fabrics. "Orion might already be at the treasure."

"Sixteen hundred and forty-seven, sixteen hundred and forty-eight," agreed Doctor Gardener with a nod. "Sixteen hundred and—"

Stepping off the paces, they crossed Forest Avenue and entered the Massey Health Club. When they emerged out the back a few moments later, smelling like old shoes and sweat, they found themselves in Civic Center Plaza, standing directly in front of Shadow Beach's brand-new city hall.

Just outside the city hall was a large, shallow fountain. But Doctor Gardener and the Hounds didn't let a little bit of water get in their way; they sloshed right through it. Then they climbed a set of stairs and entered city hall, their shoes soaking wet.

"Nineteen hundred and five," said Doctor Gardener, closing in on the treasure.

It's going to be in this building!" said Rose excitedly. Their hearts pounding, the Hounds scanned the corridor, half-expecting the treasure to be hanging from the ceiling or lying on the bare floor in a big golden pile.

"Nineteen hundred and fifty, nineteen hundred and fifty-one!" said Doctor Gardener, coming to a sudden halt. They all looked up. Before them was a polished oak door marked Shadow Beach Police Department.

"Of all the places to bury a stolen treasure!" said Alkali.

Rose hit Alkali in the ribs with her elbow. "Yeah, and look who got here first!"

Slumped against a nearby plastic trash basket was none other than Ramses Orion, looking extremely upset. "So, we caught up to you at last," Dr. Gardener said angrily. "The only reason you got here ahead of us is because we were hog-tied—by you!"

"And if you hadn't stolen those hieroglyphics to begin with, you wouldn't have been here at all," Rose added, shaking a finger at Orion. "Stealing, my friend, happens to be against the law. I'll make sure you never see a cent of Mrs. Gardener's treasure!"

Ramses Orion sighed and glanced from face to face. He looked stunned, as if someone had just clunked him on the head. "No one's going to see that treasure," he said at last. "It's gone for good. Buried under tons of concrete. This was an empty lot when Eloise stashed that gold, but it sure isn't anymore."

Everyone looked down at the floor for a long, silent moment. "Do you think the city would let us make a hole in the floor?" Alkali asked, tapping the floor with his shoes.

"Those paces we stepped off are hardly exact," said Rose. "We'd have to make more than one hole to pinpoint those coins."

"What about using your metal detector?" suggested Stanley.

Rose shook her head. "These days they embed iron rods in concrete. A metal detector like mine would be useless."

"Too bad we're not looking for the Monarch Cabin Strongbox treasure instead," said Alkali, recalling a story he'd recently read about in his favorite magazine, *True Treasure*. "That one was only buried under a wood floor."

Orion narrowed his eyes and growled, low and mean. "I'd like to tear down this whole building," he said. "And you kids with it!" He made a fist and pounded the floor. "Why'd they build this stupid place anyway?"

"Ahem!" said a big-jawed policeman, stepping out the door of the police department. He cleared his throat again and glared down at Ramses Orion. "What's this about tearing down the building?"

Orion looked up at the officer and gulped. "Nothing, nothing at all," he said. "My friends and I"—he forced a smile and motioned toward Doctor Gardener and the Hounds—"we were just, ummm, ah, playing a game!"

Rose folded her arms across her chest. "Why, we were doing nothing of the sort."

"This man is a kidnapper," said Doctor Gardener, pointing at Ramses. "He's no friend of ours."

"He tied us up," said Rose, "and stole my hieroglyphics, too."

The policeman raised a single eyebrow. "Hiero-glyphics?"

Alkali glanced down at the marble floor, sighed, then looked back up at the policeman. "It's a long story," he said. "We'll explain it all later when we come by to press charges."

The policeman bent down and pulled Orion to his feet. "Kidnapping is a serious charge," he said. "I'm afraid you'll have to come with me and answer a few questions."

Orion glared at the Hounds. "You kids had to go and ruin everything, didn't you?" He shook his head and bit at his lower lip. "And to think, I could have been rich enough to live like a king in Egypt."

The policeman looked at Orion as if he were nuts. "Come on," he said, taking him by the arm and leading him through the door into the police station. "You and I are going to have ourselves a little talk."

After Orion and the policeman were gone, Doctor Gardener patted Rose on the shoulder and smiled. "I'm sorry you kids didn't get the treasure," he said. "But, personally, I couldn't be happier with the way things have turned out. The treasure is safe and now so is my grandmother's reputation."

"I'm glad for your grandmother," said Alkali. He sighed. "Still, after all that work, it would have been nice to have gotten at least something."

"Don't you worry about that," said Doctor Gardener. "I plan to reward each one of you. After all, I owe you kids a lot."

"Reward?" said Stanley. His eyes lit up. "What

kind of reward?"

"Gold," said Doctor Gardener.

"Gold!" said Stanley.

"Sure," said Doctor Gardener. "From this day forward I'll fill any cavities you get with gold fillings—for free!"

"Cavities?" said Stanley, wincing.

Some reward! Alkali thought.

Rose was disappointed, but she tried her best to be polite. "Thanks," she said.

"Don't mention it," said Doctor Gardener, smiling. He looked down again at the floor and chuckled to himself. "Amazing! Of all things, the police department has saved my grandmother's reputation." He shook his head in disbelief. "Absolutely incredible!"

Just then the doors at the far end of the hall swung open and into the city hall limped Abner Peale, waving a white envelope over his head.

"Hey there, young Gardener," he shouted. "Don't go running off again. I've got to talk to you."

"That guy has been chasing us ever since we left Sphinx Hall," said Rose.

"What do you suppose he wants?" asked Stanley.

"We'll soon find out," said Alkali. He nodded as the old man came hobbling up. "Howdy, pardner."

Abner smiled at Alkali, then waved the envelope at Doctor Gardener. "I swear, Gardener, you're harder to catch than a greased pig."

"I'm sorry about that," said the Doctor, "but I was on an important mission."

"Well, so am I," said Mr. Peale. He handed the

envelope to Doctor Gardener. "A few months ago these turned up in our archives. They belonged to your grandmother. I think she would have liked you to have them."

The Treasure Hounds gathered around, and Doctor Gardener opened the envelope. "Oh, my!" he gasped, peering inside. "I remember seeing these on my grandmother when I was a little boy."

"Let's see," said Rose. "What are they?"

Doctor Gardener shook the contents of the envelope into his hand and out came five gold pins, all in the shape of beetles.

"What pretty gold bugs," said Alkali.

"They're scarab beetles to be exact, and quite valuable," said Mr. Peale. "They were very sacred to the Egyptians." He paused and glanced into the distance, lost for a moment in memory. "And they meant a lot, too, to your grandmother, Eloise."

Doctor Gardener smiled. "This is a wonderful gift," he said. "Now I have something to remember my grandmother by." He picked up one of the beetles and turned it over slowly. "I'll treasure this forever."

"But, Doctor Gardener," said Abner, "they're all for you. Not just that one."

"I know," said the Doctor, "but one is all I want." He held out his hand. "Rose, Stanley, Alkali, please, each of you take one."

"Wow, thanks," said Stanley.

"Yes, thank you very much," said Alkali and Rose.

"And this one is for you," said the doctor, handing the fourth gold pin to Mr. Peale. "I get the impression my grandmother was kind of special to you, too."

"Yes, she was," said Mr. Peale, accepting the pin. "Like her, Doctor Gardener, you're very generous."

Alkali looked down at his golden beetle and smiled. "Looks like everything turned out pretty well for everyone after all," he said. "Everyone, that is, but Ramses Orion."

"Where is Orion anyway?" asked Abner, looking around.

"Mr. Orion is having a little chat with the police," said Rose. "I do believe he's going to be tied up for a while—like those mummies of his."

Alkali put his arms around the shoulders of his two partners. "I know what else is like a mummy," he said.

"Oh," said Rose. "What?"

"This case," said Alkali. "Like a mummy, I'd say, it is definitely all wrapped up."

Some Real Treasures for You to Find

HOWDY, PARDNER! I'm Alkali Jones, and before the Hounds and I say good-bye we'd like to leave you with a little bonus. In the story you just read, perhaps you recall how I talked about two old treasures I'd read about: the Dutch Oven Gold and the Monarch Cabin Strongbox.

Well, these are real treasures that no one has yet found. What follows are brief descriptions of the treasures and some clues about where they might be found. Begin your search, though, in your local library. There you will find all kinds of books on treasure hunting, including more information on the two mentioned here. Who knows, maybe someday you'll be a Treasure Hound, too. Happy hunting!

THE DUTCH OVEN GOLD

In 1885, a caravan of covered wagons driven by miners grown rich in the California gold fields was attacked by outlaws while passing through some sand dunes about ten miles southwest of Offerle, Kansas (in Edwards County). When it appeared the outlaws were going to win the battle, the miners stashed the gold in a heavy iron Dutch oven and buried it in the dunes. The only survivor of the attack was a young girl. Sometime later she told the story of the Dutch oven, but the exact burial spot has never been found.

Monarch Cabin Strongbox

In the 1880s, the West was filled with gamblers, some honest and some not above a bit of cheating. Whether a gambler named Fleming was honest or not, we'll never know. What we do know is that he was able to make a small fortune in gold coins through his skillful card playing. In a letter to his sister in Cincinnati, written in the late 1880s, he told her that he had hidden a strongbox full of gold coins under the floor of his cabin, located northwest of Monarch, Montana (southeast part of Cascade County), on the banks of the tiny Bell River. In his letter he said that he would be home by spring. But on New Year's Eve, Fleming's luck ran out. A gambling dispute just outside of Great Falls, Montana, erupted in gunfire, and Fleming was killed. As far as can be determined, the strongbox has never been located. Because the cabin has probably disappeared, you will need to check old deeds and records in the town of Monarch in order to locate its probable location.